ADDISO

How the Moon Got in the Sky

A Publication of the World Language Division

Editor-in-Chief: Judith Bittinger

Project Director: Elinor Chamas

Editorial Development: Elly Schottman

Production/Manufacturing: James W. Gibbons

Cover and Text Design/Art Direction: Taurins Design
Associates, New York

Illustrator: Joanna Fabris

ISBN 0-201-19359-0
    13 14 15-WR-96 95

Addison-Wesley Publishing Company

Reading, Massachusetts • Menlo Park, California • New York • Don Mills, Ontario • Wokingham, England
Amsterdam • Bonn • Sydney • Singapore • Tokyo • Madrid • San Juan

Long ago in Africa
there was a wonderful
spider named Anansi.

Anansi had many adventures.

One night, Anansi the Spider was in the forest. He found something strange and beautiful.

t was a great circle of light.
t was shining brightly.
Anansi stared at the light.

6

"How beautiful!" said Anansi.
"I will take it home.
I will give it
to one of my six sons.
But which one?"
Anansi couldn't decide.

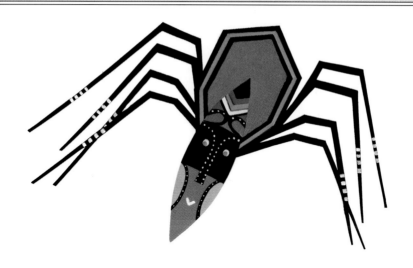

All six sons wanted
the beautiful light.
"Give it to me,"
each son said.
"Please give it to me."
Anansi still couldn't decide.

10

Anansi called to Nyame,
the God of All Things.
"Nyame, please help me.
Tell me what to do.
I want each of my sons
to be happy."

12

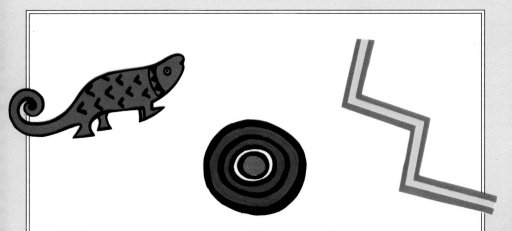

Nyame was listening.
Nyame was thinking.
Nyame finally decided
that no one person
could have the light.
Nyame reached down and
picked up the beautiful,
shiny light.

Nyame threw the light
high into the sky.
Everyone could see it.
Everyone could enjoy it.

It was beautiful then,
and it is beautiful now.
That is how the moon
got in the sky.

The End